COMPUTATION OF BATTLE

CONNOR WHITELEY

COMPUTATION OF BATTLE

No part of this book may be reproduced in any form or by any electronic or mechanical means. Including information storage, and retrieval systems, without written permission from the author except for the use of brief quotations in a book review.

This book is NOT legal, professional, medical, financial or any type of official advice.

Any questions about the book, rights licensing, or to contact the author, please email connorwhiteley@connorwhiteley.net

Copyright © 2021 CONNOR WHITELEY

All rights reserved.

DEDICATION
Thank you to all my readers without you, I couldn't do what I love.

COMPUTATION OF BATTLE

The engines roared to life.

Tarnvir gripped the cold, immense metal bar next to him as the fighter zoomed out of the ship.

His breathing quickened.

Tarnvir's rich, heavy metal armour pressed into the black metal walls of the fighter, as it picked up speed.

Sweat started to drip down Tarnvir's back.

Inside his small black helmet, he bit his lip.

Even his hands started to shake.

The smell of his own sweat and fear filled his nose.

He needed to focus.

With shaking hands holding tightly to the metal bar, Tarnvir turned to see a large silver box room in the fighter. Lined with cold unloved metal walls and black metal mesh on the floor and ceiling.

Tarnvir had no idea what it was for.

Decoration?

A few metres from him were a row of five seats on each wall but they were empty.

Tarnvir was alone.

Except for the five immense humanoid constructs.

Easily, three metres tall with cold grey metal encasing them.

Tarnvir subtly shook his head, looking upon the metal domes were human heads once laid.

He hated this part of his home regiment.

Part of him wished to be born on any other world except a Forge world. A grand planet dedicated to the sole purpose of creating war machines to fuel the Emperor's eternal war.

Although, from reports and the odd conversations his commander had allowed to him to have with off worlders. His planet was extreme in the eyes of the Empire.

Tarnvir looked down at his right hand in disgust.

Flexing the mechanical replacement of his once fleshy arm.

There was nothing wrong with his arm. Which annoyed Tarnvir even more.

He thought it was ridiculous that he had to replace his body parts with machines to serve.

All he wanted to do was kill the enemies of his Emperor.

He didn't want to replace body part after body part.

Then the memory of the cold metal barrel of a pistol against his head reminded him of the ritual where he had to choose which body part to replace.

He chose his left arm.

As punishment for hesitation, his commanders replaced his right arm.

Barbaric Tarnvir thought.

He turned his head towards the humanoid battlesuits once more.

Some within his regiment thought he was blessed for being gifted with these heroes to fight with.

Tarnvir snarled at the thought.

These humans that replaced every living part of their body until they were brain dead were not heroes.

These were failures, extremists.

Tarnvir longed for the honour of death and the ultimate escape from his strange planet and their army.

The fighter jerked.

The smell of burning oil whiffed into Tarnvir's nose.

He rolled his eyes. Hoping that the Battlesuits were malfunctioning.

He needed them.

The young officer almost laughed at the grand tales of Battlesuits and their prowess on the battlefield.

Yet Tarnvir knew these were only extreme tales to keep the soldiers replacing their weak flesh.

Regardless of his hate towards his planet and their body replacing obsession, he needed to focus on his mission.

For he was sent to do his Emperor's work despite thousands of protests.

His home world was built around the ideas of the flesh is weak and war is a science. A mere series of computations.

So, when the horrific alien abominations of the Manducare entered the orbit of a nearby mining world. Tarnvir's regiment acted.

He shook his head at the memory.

Tarnvir could still feel the blood dripping off his armour from the brutal battles he had fought.

The smoky metallic smell of the alien blood still lingered in his nose.

He could still feel the alien claws lash at his skin.

Then Tarnvir's breathing slowed to almost nothing.

The memory of thousands of ghostly Manducare swarming his allies was terrifying.

It was a simple blur.

Thousands of ghostly green aliens slaughtering thousands of humans.

Tarnvir saw his friends being hacked to pieces with ease.

He had retreated.

The computation had changed.

It was updated to accommodate this new data.

Tarnvir had a subtle laugh.

The stupidity of his home world was unbelievable.

War wasn't some computation.

War was a battle that is only decided on the battlefield.

No computation can ever be true.

Then the memory of his friends turning their backs on him as he vowed to prove them wrong.

The fighter hummed louder as it entered low orbit.

Tarnvir scratched his head.

He wasn't going to return without victory.

Not after the Commanders had almost voted him as a traitor for going against the computation.

A drop of sweat trickled down Tarnvir's cheek as he remembered the only reason he was alive was because the Lord Computation, the Leader of the Military, gave Tarnvir a chance to prove him wrong.

All Tarnvir needed to do was win a battle.

So, the Commanders ordered Tarnvir to win a battle between the local military forces and the Manducare.

His stomach churned.

He had seen the computation before he left.

Twenty percent chance of victory.

Eighty percent chance of defeat.

Three Manducare to one human soldier.

Tarnvir's stomach flipped.

He couldn't succeed, not against those odds.

The engines slowed.

The Battlesuits activated.

Moving around.

Flexing their immense staffs of electrical power in their right hands and their equally massive adamantium shields in their left.

The floor hummed open to reveal the battle ten metres below him.

The Battlesuits looked at Tarnvir.

Now was his chance.

Tarnvir jumped.

***

The Battlesuits followed.

Hissing filled Tarnvir's ears as his armour's jets activated to stop his fall.

He landed gently on the ground.

The smooth blue rock pulsed coldness through his armoured feet.

In the distance, Tarnvir saw an immense river of human soldiers in their green armour fire laser bolts into the air.

As a storm of sickly green and blue ghostly aliens descended upon the mass of human soldiers.

His heart started to beat faster.

The sky overhead turned orange as the three suns of the planetary system were slowly being devoured by the night.

Tarnvir began to walk towards the battle ahead.

His laser gun firmly in his grip.

He heard the metal cladded feet of the Battlesuits behind him.

The closer he got to the battle, the stronger the smell of burning flesh and smouldering corpses got.

Tarnvir took a deep breath as he heard the endless deafening screams of soldiers dying in their thousands.

His feet crushed the small blue peddles as he walked towards the battle.

The foul taste of death and blood formed on his tongue.

He knew the computation wasn't on his side.

Tarnvir tapped the computer screen on his right arm.

Various holographic displays formed on the inside of his helmet.

Hundreds of data streams shouted for his attention.

But he was only interested in one.
The Computation of Victory.
18% chance of victory.
Tarnvir picked up his pace.
He charged forward.
The Battlesuits followed.
Tarnvir open fired.
His laser gun unleashing a volley of laser bolts at the ghostly aliens ten metres ahead of him.
A bolt hit an alien.
It shrieked as the laser burned its ghostly flesh.
Other aliens turned around and screamed.
They zoomed towards him.
Tarnvir fired.
Multiple foes shrieked as they were burned away from reality.
One alien dived for Tarnvir.
He whipped out his silver combat sabre.
An electrical burst annihilated the alien before it could reach Tarnvir.
In all their metalic might, the Battlesuits stormed forwards.
Charging towards the swarm of aliens.
It did not matter.
12% chance of Victory.
Tarnvir followed the Battlesuits into battle.
A part of Tarnvir marvelled as the battlesuits thrusted their electrical staffs into the enemy.
Explosions of energy filled the landscape.
Aliens screamed as they were slaughtered.
Soldiers cheered as hope returned.
Tarnvir fired an endless volley of shots into the enemy.

The aliens corpses rained down upon the soldiers.

Alien blood turned the battle into sticky, stinking mud.

Tarnvir read the computation.

He beamed.

15% chance of Victory.

They threw Tarnvir to the ground.

A freezing icy claw wrap round his throat.

His neck burned with the cold.

Tarnvir focused.

A massive ghostly alien wearing black rags pinned him to the ground.

The creature pushed him into the mud.

The cold radiated through his armour.

Tarnvir's body wanted to shake.

Numbness filled his limbs.

The young Officer scratched at the ghostly arm holding his throat.

Immense pain filled his fingers as it touched the alien.

He smashed and bashed at the arm.

Tarnvir looked at the face of the alien.

It didn't have one.

It was a mere black abyss of shadow.

An electrical staff was thrusted into its chest.

The creature's chest exploded.

Tarnvir gasped.

He jumped up.

Only to see the Battlesuits being ripped limb from limb by a swarm of the aliens.

10% chance of Victory.

Tarnvir looked around.

Bright red energy radiated from the aliens.

COMPUTATION OF BATTLE

The human soldiers were firing endless streams of red laser bolts into the sky.

Yet the smell of burning flesh only grew more intense.

In the distance, thousands of corpses were being chomped upon by the Manducare.

Tarnvir's heart sank.

He had heard reports of the Manducare feasting upon the dead.

Tarnvir never expected to see it.

A loud scream caught Tarnvir's attention.

Tens of soldiers pointed to a pile of corpses to Tarnvir's left.

He wanted to scream.

His body went icy cold.

Out of the corpses of the humans spawned small ghostly aliens.

5% chance of victory.

Anyone else might have stormed over to slaughter these alien abominations.

Tarnvir froze.

The wreckage of the Battlesuits laid at Tarnvir's feet.

With shaky hands, he fired his gun once more.

Click went the trigger, click, click, click.

0% chance of Victory.

It was over.

The aliens had won.

They could create endless numbers of reinforcements from the dead.

Humanity could never win against these creatures.

The computation was right.

Victory was lost.

Tarnvir pressed a final button on his armour.

In a rough crackling voice, he ordered: "I was wrong. The Lord Computation was right. Teleport me back. Burn the world,"

https://www.subscribepage.com/garrosignup

https://www.subscribepage.com/wintersignup

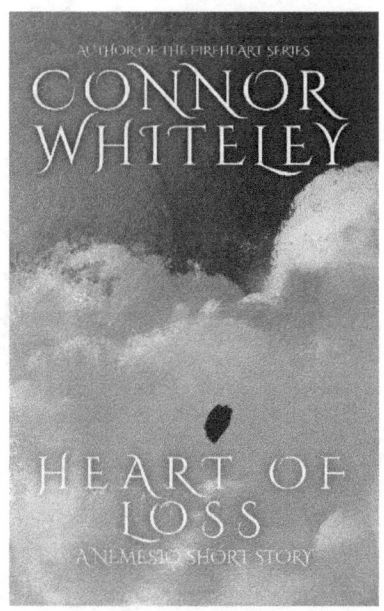

GET YOUR FREE AND EXCLUSIVE SHORT STORY NOW! LEARN ABOUT NEMESIO'S PAST!

https://www.subscribepage.com/fireheart

Thank you for reading.

I hoped you enjoyed it.

If you want a FREE book and keep up to date about new books and project. Then please sign up for my newsletter at www.connorwhiteley.net/

Have a great day.

About the author:

Connor Whiteley is the author of over 30 books in the sci-fi fantasy, nonfiction psychology and books for writer's genre and he is a Human Branding Speaker and Consultant.

He is a passionate warhammer 40,000 reader, psychology student and author.

Who narrates his own audiobooks and he hosts The Psychology World Podcast.

All whilst studying Psychology at the University of Kent, England.

Also, he was a former Explorer Scout where he gave a speech to the Maltese President in August 2018 and he attended Prince Charles' 70th Birthday Party at Buckingham Palace in May 2018.

Plus, he is a self-confessed coffee lover!

OTHER SHORT STORIES BY CONNOR WHITELEY

Blade of The Emperor

Arbiter's Truth

The Bloodied Rose

Asmodia's Wrath

Heart of A Killer

Emissary of Blood

Computation of Battle

Old One's Wrath

Other books by Connor Whiteley:

The Fireheart Fantasy Series

Heart of Fire

Heart of Lies

More Coming Soon!

The Garro Series- Fantasy/Sci-fi

GARRO: GALAXY'S END

GARRO: RISE OF THE ORDER

GARRO: END TIMES

GARRO: SHORT STORIES

GARRO: COLLECTION

GARRO: HERESY

GARRO: FAITHLESS

GARRO: DESTROYER OF WORLDS

GARRO: COLLECTIONS BOOK 4-6

GARRO: MISTRESS OF BLOOD

GARRO: BEACON OF HOPE

COMPUTATION OF BATTLE

GARRO: END OF DAYS

<u>Winter Series- Fantasy Trilogy Books</u>

WINTER'S COMING

WINTER'S HUNT

WINTER'S REVENGE

WINTER'S DISSENSION

<u>Miscellaneous:</u>

THE ANGEL OF RETURN

THE ANGEL OF FREEDOM

www.ingramcontent.com/pod-product-compliance
Lightning Source LLC
LaVergne TN
LVHW011901060526
838200LV00054B/4471